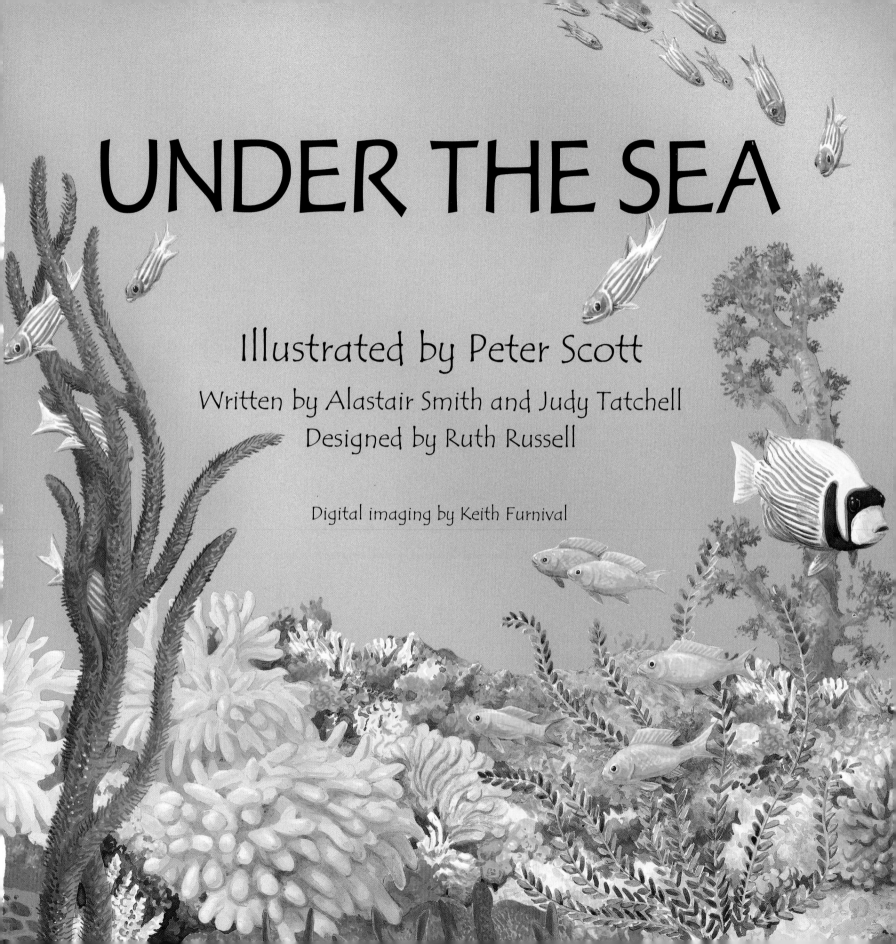

UNDER THE SEA

Illustrated by Peter Scott

Written by Alastair Smith and Judy Tatchell
Designed by Ruth Russell

Digital imaging by Keith Furnival

Dolphins

Under the sea, it's a different world...
Dolphins are some of the friendliest
animals that live there.

Here's a mother
dolphin with
her baby.
Lift the flap
to see her
talk to it.

Baby dolphins stay
with their mothers
until they are
about three
years old.

Watch this!

Dolphins love to play. They can swim so fast...

Dolphins breathe air, just like we do. They swim up to the surface for air.

They can breathe as fast as you can blink. Then they dive down again.

Dolphins live in groups. They help each other look after the babies.

Sharks

Sharks are all shapes and sizes. The smallest is the size of your hand. The biggest is as big as a bus.

This one is called a great white shark. It is fierce and strong.

If you were a fish in the sea...

...yo bet

A tiger shark

A blue shark

A reef shark

The biggest shark of all is called a whale shark. It's a gentle giant, though.

When it eats, it just opens wide...

A pygmy dwarf shark

The tiniest shark is called a pygmy dwarf shark.

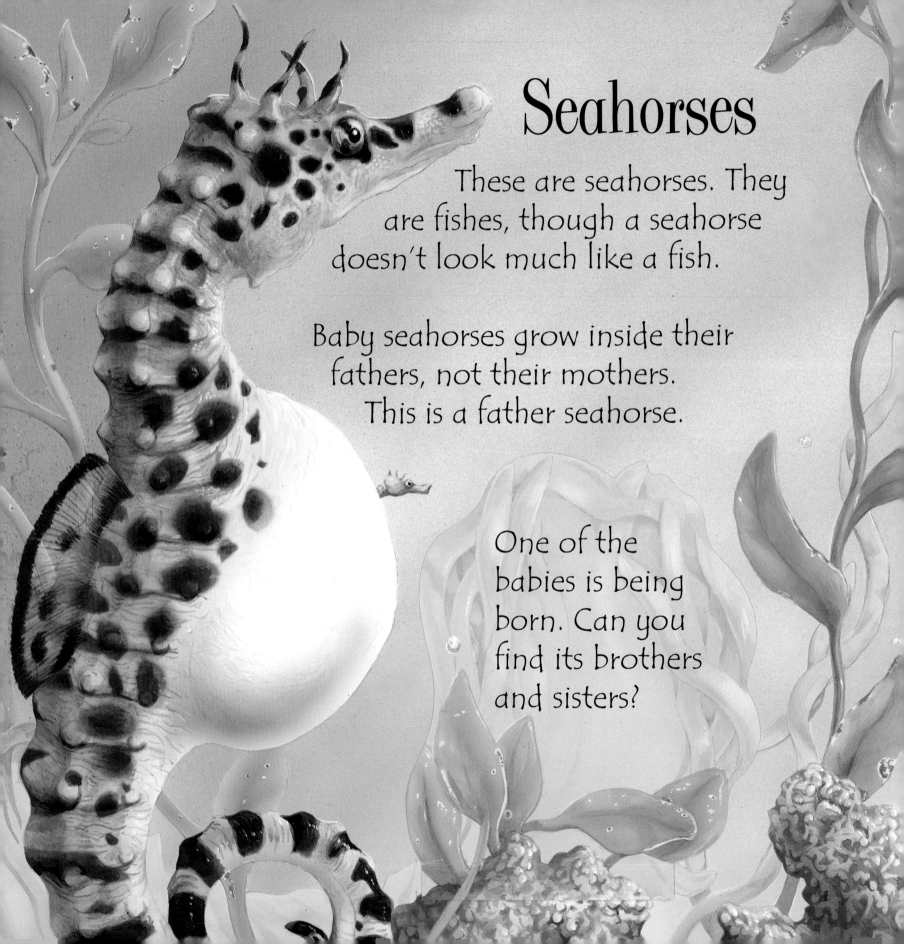

Seahorses

These are seahorses. They are fishes, though a seahorse doesn't look much like a fish.

Baby seahorses grow inside their fathers, not their mothers. This is a father seahorse.

One of the babies is being born. Can you find its brothers and sisters?

A seahorse swims by waving the fin on its back very quickly. But it still only moves along slowly.

When it wants to keep still, it curls its tail around something and holds tight.

There's another fish here, hiding in the seaweed.

All these animals are their real size. The one above isn't yet fully grown, though.

Corals

All these lovely yellow, green, blue and red shapes are made of tiny animals, called corals.

Lots of corals together like this are called a coral reef.

See what you can find living on the reef.

Lots of the fishes here have pretty patterns. This helps them to hide among the bright corals.

Corals give off a small dose of poison if something touches them. This fish is in danger!

Deep down

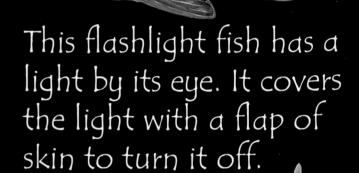

Deep in the sea it's as dark as night. Some fish have lights on them, so they can see and be seen.

This flashlight fish has a light by its eye. It covers the light with a flap of skin to turn it off.

A viper fish has a light on its back. Other fish swim to the light and get caught by the viper fish.

These are little lights.

This is an anglerfish. It has a
light above its head. Other fish
notice the light and swim to it.
But they hadter watch out...

angl

These
hairy bits
light up
too.

Near the beach

Closer to the beach, the sea is shallower. Lots of animals live here. There is plenty to eat and the water is warm.

These little things are jellyfish.

This is a blenny. There's something behind the seaweed, too.

Here, sunlight reaches the bottom of the sea, so lots of plants grow, too.

This is a sea urchin.

A starfish

These are limpets.

This stripy eel is called a zebra eel. It's chasing an octopus.

Lift the flap to see how the octopus gets away.

Fishy tricks

Some fish are good at
looking after themselves.
They use clever tricks
to keep safe
from other
hungry fish.

This puffer fish
is in danger.

This fierce fish
is a grouper.
It's looking for
something to eat.

This book has shown you some of
the things that live under the sea. But
it would take thousands of books like
this to show them all...

Additional design by Christopher Morris

First published in 2003 by Usborne Publishing Ltd, Usborne House,
83-85 Saffron Hill, London EC1N 8RT, England,
www.usborne.com
Copyright © Usborne Publishing Ltd, 2003.

Printed in China.

This parrot fish can make a gooey slime that tastes horrible.

It wraps itself up in the slime before it goes to sleep.

This is a plaice. When it's lying on sand it looks like sand. Lift the flap to see what happens if it moves.